PUFFIN BOOKS

The Dinosaur's Diary

Julia Donaldson started her career writing songs for children's television. It was only when one of her songs was made into a book, *A Squash and a Squeeze*, that she turned her hand to story-writing. She has now written over a hundred books and plays for children and teenagers, including *The Gruffalo*, which won the Smarties Prize and a Blue Peter book award. Julia lives in Glasgow with her husband Malcolm and three cats.

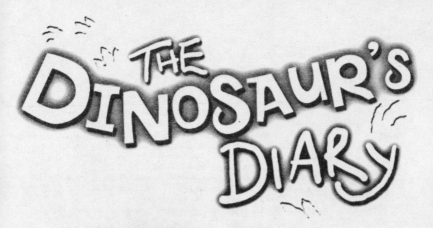

JULIA DONALDSON

Illustrated by Debbie Boon

PUFFIN

PUFFIN BOOKS

Published by the Penguin Group
Penguin Books Ltd, 80 Strand, London WC2R ORL, England
Penguin Group (USA) Inc., 375 Hudson Street, New York, New York 10014, USA
Penguin Group (Canada), 90 Eglinton Avenue East, Suite 700, Toronto, Ontario, Canada M4P 2Y3
(a division of Pearson Penguin Canada Inc.)
Penguin Ireland, 25 St Stephen's Green, Dublin 2, Ireland (a division of Penguin Books Ltd)
Penguin Group (Australia), 250 Camberwell Road, Camberwell, Victoria 3124, Australia
(a division of Pearson Australia Group Pty Ltd)
Penguin Books India Pvt Ltd, 11 Community Centre, Panchsheel Park, New Delhi – 110 017, India
Penguin Group (NZ), 67 Apollo Drive, Rosedale, North Shore 0632, New Zealand
(a division of Pearson New Zealand Ltd)
Penguin Books (South Africa) (Pty) Ltd, 24 Sturdee Avenue, Rosebank, Johannesburg 2196, South Africa

Penguin Books Ltd, Registered Offices: 80 Strand, London WC2R ORL, England

puffinbooks.com

Published 2002
12

Text copyright © Julia Donaldson, 2002
Illustrations copyright © Debbie Boon, 2002
All rights reserved

Set in 11/13 pt Garamond 3
Made and printed in England by Clays Ltd, St Ives plc

British Library Cataloguing in Publication Data
A CIP catalogue record for this book is available from the British Library

ISBN: 978-0-141-31382-5

www.greenpenguin.co.uk

Mixed Sources
Product group from well-managed
forests and other controlled sources
www.fsc.org Cert no. SA-COC-1592
© 1996 Forest Stewardship Council

FSC

Penguin Books is committed to a sustainable future
for our business, our readers and our planet.
The book in your hands is made from paper
certified by the Forest Stewardship Council.

To Madeline

Contents

T-DAY

I'm **so** excited! I'm nearly ready to lay my eggs! I had a wander round the swamp, looking for a nice safe place to lay them. That's hard, when there are so many big, fierce dinosaurs around.

It's just not fair. The biggest, fiercest dinosaurs get everything their own way. They even have days named after them. Like today – T-Day, named after Tyrannosaurus Rex, the biggest and fiercest dinosaur of all. Why can't I have a day named after me? Hypsilophodon-Day, it would be. I know that's rather a mouthful, but it could be H-Day for short.

The trouble is, I'm *not* one of the biggest fiercest dinosaurs around. Far from it. I'm nearly the smallest and one of the gentlest. I do hope I'll manage to look after my babies all right. I just can't wait to see them!

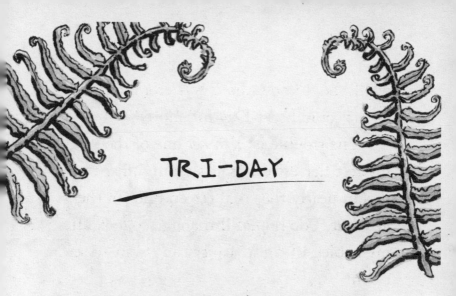

TRI-DAY

Tri-Day! I ask you! Why name a day after Triceratops? Just because she's got three horns and a fancy armour-plated frill round her neck. It's just not fair – she's tons bigger than me *and* she has all this armour to protect her against T Rex and the like.

I haven't even got *one* horn. All I've got are these two little spikes on the thumb of each of my front paws, and they're not much use.

At least Triceratops doesn't try to eat me (she only eats

plants) but she can be quite a bully. This morning I had just discovered a patch of delicious horsetail plants – my favourite food – when Tri appeared, horns lowered, saying, 'Beat it, Hypsy-Wypsy.'

It's a wonder I found anywhere to lay my eggs, but I did! Yes, I've laid them – all twenty of them! Green with black spots, like last time. I dug a hole in the mud and laid them in a beautiful spiral pattern. I covered them with bits of horsetail to keep them warm.

Oh, how I hope they'll all hatch out!

EUPH-DAY

I don't mind my friend Euphocephalus having a day named after her. She's another of these armour-plated giants, but she's not a bully like Triceratops. In fact, she's a bit of a star, especially today.

There I was, hovering round my new nest, nibbling at some lovely juicy horsetails, when all of a sudden, from out of the tall ferns, a gigantic T Rex appeared.

I froze to the spot. Normally I would run – I'm quite a nippy mover – but for some reason I couldn't bring myself to leave the nest and all my beautiful eggs.

T Rex was just about to pick me up in
his razor-sharp claws, when Euph charged
up and gave him a whack in the stomach
with the really cool club which she has at
the end of her tail. T Rex doubled up in
agony and lumbered away clutching his

stomach – he seemed to have forgotten all about me.

When I thanked Euph she just said, 'Don't mention it, old girl – you'd do the same for me.' The trouble is, I *couldn't* do the same for her – I'm just too little and all I've got to fight with are the silly spikes on my thumbs.

Thank goodness my eggs are all right!

COMP-DAY

Tragedy has struck. All my eggs have been eaten.

I was guarding the nest when T Rex appeared again. This time there was no Euph around to protect me. I forced myself to leave the nest and run for my life. I had to run for miles. It's a good job I'm so fast on my feet or I would never have got away.

But when I got back to the nest it was surrounded by a gang of Compsognathi, all smacking their jaws and licking their lips, with egg-yolk trickling down their chins.

9

I hate Comps! They are even smaller
than me, yet they have a day named after
them. I suppose it's because they go around
in a nasty, fierce gang, hunting for lizards
and insects … and dinosaur eggs.

This is just what happened to my last
lot of eggs. I am beginning to wonder if I
will *ever* have any babies. Life is very hard.

MEG-DAY, SEVERAL WEEKS LATER

Sorry about the long gap. I meant to keep this diary every day but I've been too upset. Even when I realized I was ready to lay some new eggs, I didn't feel much better.

But today has been so amazing, like some weird dream, that I simply must tell you about it.

This morning – it seems a lifetime ago! – I was wandering around *yet again* looking for a good egg-laying spot, when I heard a familiar crashing sound coming from the

tall ferns. It sounded suspiciously like T
Rex. But it wasn't. It was a Megalosaurus –
another of the awful, giant meat-eaters.

Once again, my little legs went into
action. But the ground was covered in

puddles and rocks. Meg could leap over these, but I had to splash through the puddles and dodge round the biggest rocks, which slowed me down.

I shouldn't have glanced over my shoulder but I did, and that was how I tripped over a rock. I picked myself up quickly, but I had hurt my leg. I could only limp along. This is it, I thought to myself as the footsteps behind me grew louder.

I splashed into yet another puddle and then realized that it *wasn't* a puddle – not an ordinary one, anyway. It was much deeper, more like a well. I was being sucked under the water. So I wasn't going to be eaten; I was going to drown!

But I didn't feel as if I was drowning. Strangely, I didn't seem to need to breathe at all. I closed my eyes and let the water take me down, deeper and deeper.

I felt myself being sucked around a corner, and then I was rising. Up, up, up! Faster and faster, until my head popped out of the water.

Was I in the same puddle or a different one? Was the Megalosaurus there waiting for me?

I opened my eyes and when I blinked the water out of them I found I was in some sort of pond, along with two creatures I had never seen before in my life. They were small (smaller than me!) and feathery, with beaks, and they were swimming about making what I can only describe as a quacking sound.

When they saw me, they looked terrified. Fancy anyone being terrified of *me*! Flapping like mad they half-ran, half-flew out of the water on to an island in the middle of the pond. There they stood,

beating their wings and sticking their
necks out at me angrily.

'Get out of our pond!' they quacked.

I swam to the bank and clambered
out. I took no more notice of the two
Quackosaurs, or whatever they were called,
because now I could hear another sound,

one that I didn't like at all. I looked around
me to see where it was coming from.

There was no sign of the Megalosaurus,
but in the distance I could see something
even worse. Coming towards me over some
strange-looking bumpy earth was a bright
red monster. Instead of normal legs it had
round ones that rolled across the ground.
More alarming still, it was letting out a
dreadful loud, deep roar.

I didn't stop to find out any more; I
took off. I had no idea where I was going,
and I was still limping slightly, but at least
the ground I was running over was quite
soft: it was covered in some very short
bright green plants. Where were the
horsetails? Where were the tall ferns?

After several minutes I stopped and
turned round. I could still see the big red
creature in the distance, but it didn't seem

to be coming after me. In fact it was standing still and had stopped roaring.

I could hear something else though, and it sounded like laughter – or rather, high-pitched, twittery giggling, coming from above my head.

I looked up. Some creatures with wings and forked tails were flittering about in the air. They were even smaller than the Quackosaurs – a lot smaller, in fact.

'What's so funny?' I asked them.

'You are!' said one of them cheekily. 'Fancy running away from a tractor!'

'Is that what that red monster is?' I asked. 'A – tractor, did you say? I suppose that must be short for Tractosaurus? Do you mean to say it's a plant-eater?'

The fork-tails seemed to think this was funnier than ever. They broke out into fresh twitters.

This was too much. It was bad enough feeling scared and confused without being laughed at. I felt two tears prick my eyes.

The cheeky fork-tail must have noticed, because he suddenly became very polite and said, 'Swallows here, Swinburne speaking, how may I help you?'

'I don't really know,' I answered, but then I had an idea. 'Maybe you could help me find somewhere to lay my eggs.'

'How about the henhouse?' suggested one of the swallows.

'No, not the henhouse,' said Swinburne. 'We all know what happens to the eggs in the henhouse.'

'*I* don't,' I admitted. 'What does happen to them?'

'They get boiled up for the farmer's breakfast,' said Swinburne.

'Or scrambled,' said another.

All the swallows started joining in:

'Poached.'

'Fried.'

'Coddled.'

'Made into cakes.'

'Omelettes.'

'Mayonnaise.'

This sounded terrible. I thought about the Comps. 'Do these "farmer" creatures do their egg-hunting in gangs?' I asked.

Instead of answering, Swinburne broke into another peal of twittery laughter, and the others joined in. I think this time they thought I was *trying* to be funny.

'How about the barn – that's where we lay our eggs,' said Swinburne. 'Come on and we'll show you.'

The swallows flew off together, swooping and snapping at flies. Feeling as bewildered as ever I ran after them till they reached a strange *thing.* It was rather like a huge reddish rock, but I'd never seen such a straight, square rock before.

The swallows flew through an opening right *into* the thing. I hesitated outside, but Swinburne flew out again and said, 'Come on! This is the barn!' so I followed him in.

It was dim inside the barn. I couldn't see the swallows at first, but there was a terrible din coming from above my head: 'Tweetatweet! Tweetatweetit!'

'What's been keeping you, Swinburne? Can't you hear they're starving?' came a voice. I looked up and saw a lot of saucers of mud on a high ledge. Swinburne and another swallow were perched on one of the mud saucers, out of which poked four noisy wide-open beaks.

'Meet my wife, Swoop,' said Swinburne. 'Swoop, this is . . . er . . .'

'Hypsilophodon,' I prompted him, 'but you can call me H for short.'

Swoop said nothing and gave me a funny look.

'Don't mind her,' said Swinburne. 'She's been suspicious of outsiders ever since the cat caught two of our babies last year.'

I didn't ask what a cat was – I was afraid Swinburne would laugh at me again.

'Anyway,' went on Swinburne, after he had popped some flies into the open beaks, 'this is the nesting place I was telling you about. The cat can't climb up here.'

'But neither can I,' I complained. (Swoop looked relieved.)

'How silly of me – so you can't. What about the hay loft then?' Swinburne pointed with a wing to a platform at the other end of the barn.

'But how do I get up there?' I asked.

'Try the stairs,' said Swinburne.

Do you know what stairs are? I didn't, and they looked nasty and hard and steep, but when I tried it was easy enough to get up them.

At the top I found a mound of yellow stuff which was a real treat – warm and soft to lie on, and with such a good smell that I wondered if it might be good to eat too. I nibbled a little. It wasn't bad, though not a patch on horsetails.

So that's where I am now – lying on a bed of hay (which is what the yellow stuff

is called). I'm much too tired for egg-
laying, so I'll have a sleep and think about
eggs in the morning.

What a day!

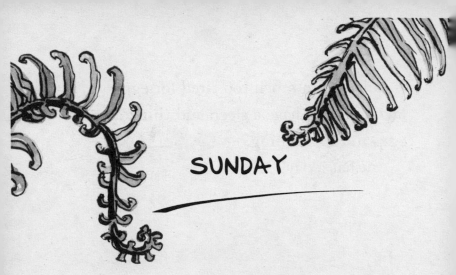

SUNDAY

The days have different names here, I've discovered. They're not named after dinosaurs like they are back home. Today is named after the sun. Most peculiar.

The main news is that I'VE LAID MY EGGS. Just wait till I tell you where! But first I must tell you about this morning.

I woke with a start. The swallows were making a dreadful racket – not their usual twittering but a shriller, louder, panicky-sounding 'Twhit! Twhit! *Twhit!*' It sounded like some kind of warning, and

immediately I realized that that's just what
it was, because I could hear something else
– the sound of heavy footsteps on the stairs!

I scrabbled under the hay just in time,
and kept completely still. Someone or
something started rummaging around in
the hay. I prayed that it wasn't a meat-

eating dinosaur. Surely whoever it was must be able to hear my heart thumping.

To my relief the rummaging stopped and I heard the footsteps disappear down the stairs.

I peeped out of the hay just in time to see a creature with floppy-looking blue skin walking out of the barn on its hind legs.

'Who was that?' I asked.

'The farmer,' said Swinburne.

'The *farmer*!' But that was the dreaded egg-eater, wasn't it? 'Oh no – was he looking for eggs?'

'You are funny, H,' said Swinburne. 'No, he was just getting some hay.'

'But I can't lay my eggs here if this farmer creature is going to keep nosing around,' I said.

'No, I suppose not,' said Swinburne. 'Sorry about that. Maybe the junk corner

would be a better place. The farmer hardly
ever goes there. Come and see what you
think.'

I lumbered down the stairs (which was
much trickier than getting up them) and
followed Swinburne to a dark corner of the
barn. At first I couldn't see much, but as
my eyes grew used to the dim light I began
to make out a jumble of strange objects.

'These are all the old broken things the farmer doesn't need – forks, spades, rakes, wheelbarrows . . .'

I didn't take in any more because at that second I saw something which made me tremble all over. It was a monster like the one I saw yesterday on the lumpy earth, only this one was brown instead of red.

'Help! A Tractosaurus!' I squealed. I ran all the way back to the hay loft and buried myself again. It was a long while before Swinburne could persuade me to come out.

Trying not to laugh, he told me that a Tractosaurus (or tractor, as he insists on calling it) isn't actually alive at all; it's something called a machine, whatever that is. It doesn't eat animals or plants; it just likes a drink called diesel but it can't drink that all by itself – the farmer has to feed it.

I still wasn't convinced. 'But I saw the other one, the red one, running around and roaring.'

'That's because the farmer was driving it. But he can't drive this one. It's all old and rusty. It doesn't work any more. That's why it's in the junk corner.'

At last I plucked up courage to go back. Sure enough, the Tractosaurus didn't move when Swinburne perched on it or even when he giggled, flew above it and spattered it with some white stuff.

Feeling very brave, I reached out with one of my front legs and touched the Tractosaurus gently. It felt cold and hard.

'I still don't think this is a good nesting place,' I said. 'What I'd really like would be some nice mud.'

'Mud!' exclaimed Swinburne. 'Really, H, why didn't you say so before? We can

find you plenty of that. Come on, mob, off to the pond!' he called out to the other swallows. 'You wait there, H.'

Before I could reply, the barn was a flurry of activity. The swallows had flown off their own nests and were helping to build mine!

In and out of the barn they flew. They flew out with empty beaks; when they returned their beaks were full of mud. Mind you, one swallow's beakful is not much mud at all, but there were so many of them and they worked so fast that it soon mounted up. What bothered me was *where* it was mounting up – inside the Tractosaurus itself!

'No – not there!' I tried to tell them, but they took no notice. The rusty old Tractosaurus was to be the home for my eggs, and that was settled. Before long I had quite come round to the idea myself.

Swoop didn't join in the mud-collecting: she stayed near her nest and looked quite disapproving, I thought. One of her babies had learned to fly but she wouldn't let him join in either. 'The cat might get you,' she told him, but I couldn't help wondering if it was really *me* she was scared of.

I must say, the mud-collectors did a brilliant job. Before long the inside of the Tractosaurus was looking lovely and squelchy, just like the swamp back home. Not at all afraid any more, I climbed up on to it. The swallows flew back to their nests; they knew that I would want to lay my eggs in private.

Swinburne was the last to leave. 'Do let me see them when you've finished,' he whispered. 'I promise I won't bring the mob with me.'

I dug into the mud – not too deep – squatted down, and at long last laid my eggs! Only thirteen of them this time, but if anything even more beautiful than the last lot.

I called softly to Swinburne. To my surprise, Swoop flew down with him. I hope she is beginning to come round to me a bit now that I have proved myself to be an egg-layer like her. But she didn't look too impressed.

'Hmm, thirteen – unlucky number,' she muttered.

'Aren't they a wonderful green?' I said. 'And don't you just love the black spots?'

'Er, yes – very nice,' said Swinburne, sounding a bit doubtful.

'They're certainly extremely *bright*,' said Swoop. 'Mine were white with pale brown speckles,' she added proudly.

Privately I thought, How dull, but I didn't say so.

Swoop flew back to her own nest, but Swinburne stayed and helped me cover the eggs up with bits of hay.

'Are you going to sit on them now?' he asked. I explained that I couldn't do that for fear of crushing them, but that I would stay close by.

'You'll need a bed, then,' said Swinburne, and he helped me fetch some more hay and spread it out on the floor beside the Tractosaurus.

'Thank you,' I said, and lay down gratefully.

I feel exhausted, but proud and happy. I have some new friends, a nice safe nest and some beautiful eggs. How, oh how I hope that this time they will hatch out and I will become a mother at last!

MONDAY

Swinburne told me that this day is named after the moon. I asked him why none of the days are named after dinosaurs. He just laughed at me again and said that dinosaurs don't *exist* here – apart from me, of course. Can this be true or is it just one of Swinburne's jokes?

TUESDAY

Tuesday is named after some ancient god called Tiu – don't ask me why.

Two more of Swinburne's and Swoop's babies learned how to fly today. Swinburne is very proud of them, but Swoop seems a bit nervous. I think it's still partly *me* she's nervous of – in her head she knows I am harmless, but in her heart she is still half afraid that I plan to attack her babies, like the cat did last year.

What sort of creature is this dreaded Catosaurus? (I assume that is what 'cat' is

short for.) I imagine a cross between T Rex and Megalosaurus.

The last baby swallow still sits in the nest going 'Tweetatweetit!' all day long and being fed beakfuls of flies.

I hope my babies will be a bit quieter and not so greedy. Oh, I can't wait for them to be born!

WEDNESDAY

Today is named after someone called Woden, who I gather is the god of farming. Apparently this place is called a farm, so I suppose that's not so silly as some of their names for days.

I've seen a cat at last! What a surprise — she is no bigger than me! But the swallows are all terrified of her, and I must say there *is* something scary about her glinting green eyes and sharp-looking claws.

I crouched on my straw watching her as *she* crouched on the floor watching the

42

swallows. They were zipping in and out on their fly-catching expeditions.

Every time a swallow flew a bit low the cat would raise her back end and wiggle it, ready to pounce. Once or twice she *did* pounce, but the swallows – even the baby ones – were too quick for her. She'd better not try pouncing on *my* babies when they're born.

THURSDAY

This day is named after the god of thunder, and today there *was* a thunderstorm, a really dramatic one. Something else dramatic happened too.

I was watching Swinburne and Swoop trying to teach the last baby how to fly, when the sky grew dark. The swallows took no notice: they went on saying, 'One, two, three, jump!' and the baby perched on the edge of the nest kept on saying, 'Not quite yet!'

Maybe the first flash of lightning

dazzled the baby swallow or maybe the first thunderclap startled him into losing his balance.

The next three things happened as quickly as another flash of lightning: the baby bird fell out of the nest, the cat streaked into the barn and seized him in her mouth, and *I* rushed out of the junk corner and charged at the cat!

It was instinct. I didn't have time to plan it or to feel afraid. But the cat got the fright of her life. When she spun round and saw me her fur stood on end and her green eyes widened as if she'd seen a ghost. She dropped the baby swallow and tore out of the barn in another blinding flash of lightning.

I raced after her, suddenly enjoying myself tremendously. Over the short green

plants I chased her, and round the pond, startling the Quackosaurs. I was so close behind her that I could have caught her tail in my mouth, but I didn't want to do that; I just wanted to make sure she stayed really frightened, so that she wouldn't think about sneaking back into the barn.

What a change this was! Me, gentle little Hypsilophodon, chasing *after* someone instead of being chased!

The sky flashed and crashed and the rain came pelting down, drenching us both, but I didn't mind. On and on we ran. We only stopped when we reached a tree. The cat shinned up it and I stood at the bottom glaring at her as fiercely as I knew how. As far as I know she's still there, too scared to come down.

When I got back to the barn I was given the welcome of my life. The swallows flew round me in circles, congratulating me and offering me flies (which I politely refused – I can't think of anything more disgusting).

Swinburne promised he would never laugh at me again and I pretended to believe him. The rescued baby, who had got over his shock, fluttered over and perched on my head. 'I think I can fly now,' he said. 'But please, please, will you teach me how to run like you?'

But the most delighted swallow of all was Swoop. 'Thank you! Thank you! You saved my baby!' she kept twittering.

Suddenly I remembered the time that Euphocephalus back home had saved *my* life.

'Don't mention it, old girl,' I said to Swoop. 'You'd do the same for me.'

FRIDAY,
SEVERAL WEEKS LATER

This day is named after Frigga, the goddess of love. And that makes sense to me, because today I'm bursting with love myself. Can you guess who for? Here's a clue: there are thirteen of them. Yes! My new babies! They hatched out this morning!

I can't get over how tiny they are, right down to their sweet little toenails and the miniature spikes on their front paws. They are a lovely browny-green colour – well, the same colour as me, actually – and they all

seem to love eating hay. Oh, I'm so happy!

I have chosen names for all the babies:
the girls are Henrietta (she is the biggest
one), Hermia, Hilda, Hannah, Hetty, Holly
and Hope. The boys are Hardy, Humphrey,
Hector, Howard, Hugh and Horace. Horace
is quite a bit smaller than all the others but
just as adorable.

Swinburne and Swoop came to admire the new arrivals, though I'm not sure if *admire* is quite the right word. They made all the right noises, but Swoop said, 'They're very nice, H, but what a shame they don't have feathers.' What a horrible thought! My babies are just perfect the way they are.

SATURDAY

This day is named after yet another god, one called Saturn, who went around eating his own children! It makes me shiver to think of it.

My own children are only a day old but already they are romping around like nobody's business. I'm so scared that the farmer will discover them.

Today I had another visitor – the baby swallow I rescued, who has had a crush on me ever since. He is called Songo, after a place in Africa where the swallows spend

every winter. Songo said it would soon be time for them to go there.

'Will you come with us, H? Please! *Please!* You can bring the babies if you like.'

But that's impossible. Apparently Africa is thousands of miles away, across a sea.

SUNDAY – A WEEK LATER

Sorry about another gap, but looking after the babies has been a full-time job.

They have now learned to climb the stairs – all except one of them, little Horace. To tell the truth, I am a bit worried about Horace – as well as being so small, he's much slower than the others.

The most advanced baby is Henrietta. In fact, I am convinced she is a genius.

Henrietta is fascinated by the controls of the Tractosaurus. Today, when she was up in the hay loft, she discovered a little

rusty object which Swinburne told her was
the starting key. She immediately took it
downstairs in her mouth, poked it into a
hole in the Tractosaurus and started
wiggling it about. Of course the
Tractosaurus didn't start (thank goodness!)
because it is old and broken.

When I told Henrietta about the other Tractosaurus, the big red one that the farmer drives, her eyes grew round with longing. But I told her she must never, *never* go anywhere near it. I don't think she took a blind bit of notice: all she said was, 'Stop calling it a Tractosaurus, Mum – it's a tractor. You're so old-fashioned.'

Oh, it is so hard being a mother! I want so desperately to protect all thirteen of them, but they are getting more adventurous every day.

MONDAY

We are just about to set out on a big adventure! We are going out to eat grass! (That is the name of the short green plant that is so common here.)

The babies have been guzzling the hay in the barn at an alarming rate. They can't carry on like that or the farmer will notice and get suspicious.

So we are going to go out and graze at night, when the farmer isn't around. We will have to be back in the barn before daylight.

The babies are all very excited. I can't help feeling scared, but I mustn't let them see that. The swallows have told me that there are some night-time hunters — creatures called owls and foxes — but apparently they are quite small, nothing like T Rex or Meg. If we all stick together in a herd we should be safe.

TUESDAY

The grazing expedition was a success.
It was a beautiful night with a full moon,
just like the one that shines over the swamp
back home. The only other animals we met
were some white woolly ones, which ran
away from us making a silly bleating noise.

The babies were quite good about
sticking together, all except Henrietta, who
kept trying to wander off in search of the
red Tractosaurus. I told her off and she
answered, 'Stop nagging, Mum!' but when
I told her that the farmer locks it up at

night she believed me and gave up.

As for the grass, the babies are potty about it and can't wait to go out again tonight.

'If you like grass, you should try horsetails!' I told them, once we were back in the barn. Of course that led to the usual cries of, 'Tell us about horsetails!', 'Tell us about T Rex!', 'Tell us about Triceratops!' They love to hear stories about the swamp, and so do the swallows. By far the favourite story is the one about Euph whacking T Rex with the club at the end of her tail.

'I want to meet Euph!' said Henrietta. 'Can't we go back there, Mum? Oh, please!'

'I don't know,' I said.

'Oh, go on! Go on! Say yes! Don't be so mean!' Henrietta went on and on. I'm sure I never pestered *my* mother like that.

When I told her there weren't any

Tractosauruses in the swamp she eventually
shut up.

'If you ever do go, I want to go with
you,' said Songo, the baby swallow, from
his usual place on top of my head. He had
been sitting there listening to the stories.

'Don't be silly,' Swoop told him.
'You're coming to Africa with us next
week.'

I hadn't realized the swallows were

going so soon. We will all miss them. I wonder if we'll still be here when they get back next spring. We can't stay here for ever. The farmer would be bound to discover us, and then what? Swinburne has told me about a horrible place called the zoo where animals are kept in cages and people come and stare at them. I dread that happening to us.

But how would we get back to the swamp? And would it be such a good idea anyway? I can't bear the thought of any of my babies being caught by T Rex or Meg. Poor little Horace is still very small and slow. It would be different if only we had some good weapons or armour, like Tri or Euph do. But all we've got are our useless thumb spikes.

Oh, the worry of it all!

WEDNESDAY

Disaster! I am one baby short. Yes, one of my precious little ones has been caught by the farmer!

I blame myself, though it all happened because Henrietta was so determined to see the red Tractosaurus.

She'd been in a strange mood all night. While the rest of us were grazing she spent a lot of time collecting sheep's wool from the hedges. (The sheep are the silly white creatures.)

'Don't be silly – you can't eat that!' I

told her, but she just ignored me.

When it was time to round up the babies and go back to the barn I noticed we were one short. Henrietta wasn't there. I called her but there was no answer.

The sun was rising and it was going to be a lovely day. Swinburne had told us that around this time of year the farmer would be starting work extra early, to begin on something called the 'harvest', which meant cutting down loads of plants. Any minute now he could be out in the fields.

It wasn't difficult to guess what Henrietta was up to — she must have sneaked off to hide and catch a glimpse of the famous red Tractosaurus that she couldn't get out of her mind.

I felt torn. I didn't want to keep the others out a minute longer. We'd wandered quite a way from the barn and it would

take longer than usual to get back –
especially for little Horace. Perhaps the
sensible thing to do would be to go back to
the barn with them, but I couldn't bear to
leave Henrietta alone and in danger.

'You run back,' I told the others. 'You
know the way to the barn. I'll look for
Henrietta.'

It didn't take very long to find her. It
was the sheep that gave away her hiding
place. A lot of them were clustered in the
corner of the field bleating extra loudly. I
went over to investigate. They didn't run
away – they've got used to us now. They
seemed much more interested in one of the
lambs, a rather strange, patchy-looking one.

Wait a second! That wasn't a lamb at
all. In between the patches of wool I could
see browny-green skin – skin that I
recognized. Dinosaur skin!

'Henrietta!' I said.

'Oh, Mum, why do you have to spoil everything?' said Henrietta.

She had rolled in some mud and then plastered herself with the sheep's wool that she had been collecting.

'What on earth did you do that for?' I asked.

'So the farmer won't spot me, of course,' said Henrietta. 'I'm not stupid, Mum, though you seem to think so. I must see the red tractor, I must, I *must*!'

'It's coming now!' said one of the sheep.

And sure enough, I could hear in the distance the dreadful roar that had scared me so much the day I arrived here. The red Tractosaurus was out, and it was coming our way!

'Quick, Henrietta, run!' I said.

But Henrietta wouldn't. And I realized there was more chance that we would be spotted if we *did* run. The farmer probably wouldn't notice Henrietta surrounded by sheep and covered in wool. I was in more danger of being seen than she was. But

Henrietta ordered the sheep to cluster round me – she seems to have quite a way with them.

The noise grew louder. I crouched down and prayed I was blending in with the grass as the big red beast (yes, I know it's not a beast really but I can't stop thinking of it as one) came roaring past us. The farmer was sitting inside it, dressed in his strange floppy skin – sorry, clothes – holding the steering wheel and singing a song.

Henrietta was transfixed. 'It's *wonderful*!' she said. 'Oh, how I'd love to drive it!'

She sighed with longing. As for me, I sighed too – with relief. But relief was not what I should have been feeling, as I was soon to find out.

When we returned to the barn we were greeted by eleven anxious babies – yes, eleven, not twelve. They were all talking at once.

'Horace!'

'He was so slow!'

'He couldn't keep up!'

'He still hasn't got back!'

'He must be lost!'

'Or hurt!'

But Horace wasn't lost or hurt. I know that now, because the swallows organized a search party. It was little Songo who brought back the terrible news.

'Horace is in the farmhouse,' he told us.
'I looked through the window. He's in a
sort of basket with bars.'

'That sounds like the cat basket!' said
Swinburne knowledgeably.

At that moment everything started
spinning round and my knees gave way.
The next thing I knew I was lying on the
barn floor covered in swallows who were
fanning me with their wings. Little Songo,

perched on my head, was fanning up a
hurricane. My own babies were gathered
round anxiously.

'You fainted, Mum,' Henrietta told me.
'But you'll be fine, and so will Horace.
We're going to rescue him!'

'But why is he in the cat basket?' I
asked. 'Is the farmer going to feed him to
the cat?'

'No,' said Swinburne. Usually he
laughs at my mistakes, but things were too
serious. 'But maybe he's planning to take
him to the vet. Songo, I want you to fly
straight back to the farmhouse and find out
all you can. Watch what the farmer does
and listen to anything he says.'

'What's a vet?' I asked faintly when
Songo had flown off. 'Is it a kind of zoo?'

'No, the vet is a person who knows a
lot about animals and looks after them

when they're ill,' Swinburne told me. 'Sometimes he comes to the farm. I saw him sticking a needle into one of the sheep once.'

That sounded dreadful! But I knew that even worse things could happen to animals – they could be eaten, or locked up. I wanted to charge to the farmhouse then and there and defend my baby. But Swoop talked me out of it.

'I know just how you feel, my dear,' she said, 'but it wouldn't be wise. Wait till our Songo gets back with some more news and then we can decide what to do.'

So we waited. And waited. It was getting dark by the time Songo flew into the barn and back on to my head.

'Horace is all right so far,' he told us. 'But I heard the farmer talking to someone on the telephone.' (Whatever that is.) 'He's planning to take Horace somewhere in the car tomorrow.'

'Do you know at what time?'
Swinburne asked.

'Yes – half past eleven. He said that
would be a good time to take a break from
the harvesting.'

'What's a car?' I asked, and was
horrified to learn that it was something like
a Tractosaurus but much faster.

'Does it have tyres?' Henrietta asked, and
her eyes lit up when she learned that it did.
I turned on her then. 'How can you be
getting all excited about a machine at a
time like this?' I said to her. 'Don't you
realize that your little brother's life is in
danger?' And then – perhaps unfairly – I
added, 'And what's more, you got him into
this danger!'

'Yes,' said Henrietta, 'and I'm going to
get him out of it!'

Songo looked worried. 'I don't see how,' he said. 'I flew all round the farmhouse looking for a way in, but all the doors and windows were shut.'

'Never mind that,' said Henrietta. 'Just tell me if there's somewhere near the farmhouse we could hide for the night.'

'What, all of you?'

'Yes. It has to be somewhere where we can see the farmer but he can't see us.'

Songo thought for a minute. 'I know,' he said. 'There's a big haystack in the field next to the house. Maybe you could hollow it out and hide in there.'

I felt I was being left behind. 'But we don't *all* need to go, surely?' I asked.

'Yes, Mum, we do,' said Henrietta. 'As soon as you and I have rescued Horace we all need to be ready to run.'

'To run where?'

'Somewhere, anywhere – but not back to the barn. We can't stay here any longer, it's just too dangerous.'

'There are some woods across the road from the farm – maybe you could go there,' suggested Swinburne.

'But I don't want you to go!' said Songo. 'If you do go, I'm going with you!'

'No,' said Swoop, gently but firmly. 'You're coming to Africa with us, remember? The woods would be too cold for you in winter.'

'But how are we going to rescue Horace?' I asked Henrietta.

'Don't worry, Mum – I'm working on it,' was all she would say.

What on earth is she planning? And what is the farmer planning to do with Horace? Whatever it is, we must stop him!

THURSDAY

Why did I ever complain about the spikes on my front paws? I thought they were pretty useless weapons, but today has proved me wrong.

Today has also proved what a star Henrietta can be. Yes, she's strong-willed; yes, she's disobedient; yes, she can be pretty rude to me, but when it comes to planning a rescue operation you couldn't beat her.

The babies enjoyed hollowing a tunnel through the haystack and snuggling inside it. The swallows tidied up the hay we'd

scooped out. They built some of it into a kind of screen at the front of the tunnel, so that no one could see us.

The screen of hay was quite thin, though, and we could see out. We could see the farmhouse (where the farmer lives), the tractor shed (where the red Tractosaurus lives) and the dreaded car which stood outside. Actually, the car didn't look too scary – it was a lot smaller than the Tractosaurus – but Swinburne says it can run even faster than *me* when the farmer is inside it.

We tried to sleep while the swallows kept watch.

Early in the morning the farmer came out of his house, took the Tractosaurus out of the shed and drove off to the fields.

'He's out of sight,' twittered Swinburne.

'Off we go, Mum,' said Henrietta.

The two of us crept out of the haystack.
The others wanted to come too but we
wouldn't let them. It was too risky.

Henrietta and I trotted over to the car,
which was glinting blue in the new
daylight.

Henrietta's eyes glinted too when she
had a close look at the tyres.

'*No* sweat!' she said. 'One, two, three,
jab!' and she hit out at a front tyre with
both front paws.

I watched in horrified fascination, almost expecting the car to hit back, but it kept quite still.

'Come on, Mum! This is fun!' said Henrietta.

I couldn't let her see I was half afraid of the car, so I lashed out at the other front tyre. It was most satisfying to feel my two spikes puncture the black rubber. I fancied I could hear a faint hiss.

'Keep going!' Henrietta encouraged me.

Before long we had jabbed all four tyres all over.

Then it was back to our haystack cave to wait for the farmer's return. Once again the swallows sealed the entrance with hay.

The babies liked being in a house they could eat, but I was too nervous to nibble at the hay. I felt quite sick when I peeped out and saw the farmer returning, on foot.

this time, and going inside the farmhouse.

I felt sicker still when he came out again. He was carrying an arch-shaped basket with bars across the front. And cowering inside the basket, his eyes wide with fear, was my little Horace.

'No! Stop!' I cried. I would have charged out of the haystack and attacked the farmer but Henrietta restrained me.

'Stick to the plan, Mum,' she whispered urgently.

The farmer put the basket down on the seat beside him and started up the car.

It made a loud noise and, to my horror, began to move forward.

'It's all right, Mum!' hissed Henrietta, sensing that I was again on the point of rushing out of the haystack. And sure enough, the car stopped and we heard the farmer cursing and muttering.

He got out of the car and inspected the tyres. He cursed a lot louder then, and stormed off into the house. Songo flew to the window to spy on him.

'Now!' said Henrietta.

I *did* race out of the haystack then, and round to the driver's door of the car. It was open. I leaped inside, and Henrietta leaped after me.

'Mum!' squeaked Horace, pressing his nose against the bars of his basket.

There was no time to talk to him: I needed my mouth for something else.

Songo had explained to me how the bars were fixed to the basket with two things called leather straps, and I knew what to do – gnaw. I set to work on one of the straps while Henrietta gnawed away at the other one.

Songo fluttered to the car door.

'You're all right still,' he said. 'The
farmer's talking to someone on the
telephone.'

I gnawed for all I was worth. The leather was quite tough (I found out afterwards it's made from animal skin – horrible thought) but my teeth were tougher. I gnawed through my strap and finished off Henrietta's one. Then I hooked the barred door open and out crept Horace! He snuggled up to me on the car seat, and I could feel him trembling.

'No time for cuddles,' Henrietta warned us, and at the same time we heard a shrill 'Twhit! Twhit!' which was the swallows' warning call. The farmer was coming out of his house!

'Run!' hissed Henrietta.

We leaped out of the car and ran towards the haystack, Henrietta leading the way. I followed her with Horace. He was so slow! Had the farmer seen us or not? I didn't turn round to find out.

We reached the haystack and dived inside. Only then did I allow myself to turn round and peep out. The farmer *couldn't* have seen us; I'd have heard his feet chasing after us if he had.

But he *had* seen us. He was standing by the car holding the empty basket and staring goggle-eyed at the haystack. He looked as if he was frozen to the spot.

He unfroze pretty quickly, though, and started to run our way. He wasn't what I'd call fast, but then neither was Horace.

'Back door!' ordered Henrietta. We'd dug our tunnel right through to the other side of the haystack, and we now jostled each other to escape that way. Henrietta quickly overtook the others and led the way. Horace and I were lagging behind, and this time I *could* hear the farmer's feet behind us.

Where was Henrietta leading us? We couldn't go to the wood after all, at least not the most direct way – it would mean running back past the farmer.

I was soon to find out.

We rounded a hedge, and there in the middle of the next field stood the red Tractosaurus. Henrietta was bounding towards it, the other babies hot on her heels.

Horace and I were way behind, and the farmer was hot on *our* heels. I could hear him panting now. Any second and he would make a grab for one of us. This is it! I thought. I'll have to turn round and fight.

But what was this I could hear? A tremendous twittering was drowning out the farmer's panting. I sneaked a glance over my shoulder. The farmer had stopped

running. He stood still, surrounded by a cloud of swallows. They were circling him, swooping and flittering, twittering madly. The farmer was flapping his front paws, trying to beat them off.

'Mum! Horace! Hurry up!' Henrietta's voice sounded different, as if she was speaking through clenched teeth.

I looked ahead again, and saw that Henrietta was actually *in* the red Tractosaurus, behind the steering wheel. In her mouth was a key. The other babies were clambering in and clustering round her. What were they up to?

There was no time to wonder. Horace managed a burst of speed and I followed him. Two of the other babies reached down and helped Horace up on to the Tractosaurus. I leaped on behind him.

Henrietta slotted the key into a hole

beside the wheel; she'd practised this often enough on the rusty Tractosaurus in the barn. But this time it was different. The red Tractosaurus let out a deep growl, scaring me out of my wits.

'Handbrake off, Hardy! Step on the gas, Hermia!' Henrietta was giving orders to two of the other babies. The Tractosaurus lurched and moved forward. We were off!

The things I remember most about that scary, bumpy journey are sounds – I think I must have had my eyes closed in fright, because I don't remember any *sights* at all. I could hear the Tractosaurus's roar, the farmer's shouts and curses and the excited twittering of the swallows.

And then there was another sound – an alarmed quacking which I just had time to recognize as the Quackosaurs' noise before

there came the most terrifying sound of all
– a loud splash.

H-DAY

Yes, you read it right. H-Day! At last I have a day named after me.

And I didn't think I would live to see another day – any sort of day. Not when I heard that splash yesterday and realized what had happened. Henrietta had driven the Tractosaurus into the pond!

The babies couldn't swim – not as far as I knew, anyway. I could a bit, but I certainly wasn't going to save myself and let them drown.

But perhaps you've guessed what

actually happened. It was like the
time I was being chased by Meg,
only in reverse. We sank down and
down, Tractosaurus and babies and
all, without needing to breathe.
Then it was round a corner and up,
up, up! And there we were, still
inside the Tractosaurus, but no longer
in the pond or even on the farm. No, we
were back home!

Of course, I didn't realize this at first,
as my eyes were still closed. That is, until I
heard Henrietta squeal, 'Look! A
Megalosaurus!' I opened them then.

It was, too – and I could swear it was
the same one that had chased me into the
puddle. But this time he didn't look in
the mood for doing any chasing. I
have never seen such an expression
of terror, except perhaps on

the cat's face back in the barn.

I'm sure Meg didn't recognize me; he obviously thought that the babies and I were all part of the terrifying Tractosaurus.

'After him!' shouted Henrietta, who was still at the wheel. The babies in charge of the other controls obeyed her, and the Tractosaurus lurched noisily forward again.

Meg ran for his life. Actually, he wasn't in danger, as the Tractosaurus isn't all that fast, but he wasn't taking any chances. Soon he was just a blob in the swampy distance.

We carried on for a minute or two, till I spotted the most wonderful patch of horsetails. Henrietta parked the Tractosaurus by some tall ferns and we all bounded out.

I can't tell you how delicious that first

mouthful of horsetails tasted, after so many weeks of hay and grass. The babies obviously agreed. Horace, in particular, was tucking in with a speed and enjoyment I'd never seen before. I could almost see him putting on weight.

We were munching away so blissfully
that we didn't hear Triceratops lumbering
up behind us.

'These are *my* horsetails, Hypsy-Wypsy,'
she growled, all three horns lowered.

I was about to clear off, but Henrietta,

cool as a cucumber (whatever that is — I picked up the expression from Swinburne), answered: 'Share and share alike, Tri. After all, we're sharing with our friend here,' holding back a fern to reveal the Tractosaurus in all its glory. One glance was enough for Tri. She was off, her silly armour-plated frill quivering in terror.

'All brawn and no brain,' came a voice which I was sure I recognized. I turned and saw a familiar head rearing out of a hollow in the swamp.

'Well, H, aren't you going to introduce *me* to your new friend?'

It was my old friend Euph. And clustered around her were a dozen babies, each with a miniature club at the end of its tail!

My own babies were green with envy (well, they were green already, but you

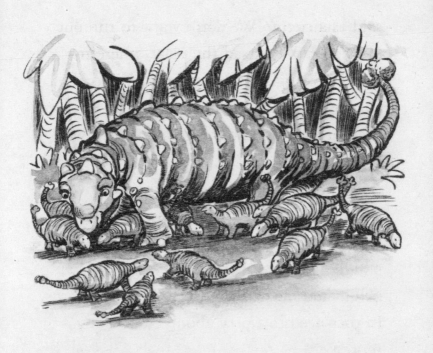

know what I mean). They all wanted clubs
too. But Euph's babies seemed to think that
the Tractosaurus was better than any
number of clubs, and begged to be taken
for a ride.

So Euph and I conducted a guided tour
of the swamp – 'Just a short one, though,'

said Henrietta. 'We don't want to run out of diesel.' We passed the place where my last lot of eggs had been eaten by the Compsognathi after I'd fled from T Rex; we even saw a T Rex, but as soon as he saw *us* he ran a mile.

Oh, it's so good to be home, to have all thirteen babies alive (if you ask me, thirteen is a lucky number, not an unlucky one like Swoop said), and to have our own bright red metal armour – the Tractosaurus. I don't need to worry about Horace any more.

Talking of Horace, he is turning out to be a wonderful storyteller. This evening Euph and her babies sat and listened for hours to his tales about the farmer and the cat basket and, of course, the swallows.

We do miss the swallows. But we wouldn't have seen much more of them.

They're probably on their way to Africa by now. Perhaps they'll tell stories about *us* to the other birds and animals they meet there.

'It's sad to think we'll never see them again,' I said to Henrietta today after all the others had gone to sleep.

But Henrietta just gave me a funny look.

'They're coming back, you know,' she said. 'They only stay in Africa for half the year. And we'll be needing more diesel.'

I have a feeling that in half a year's time Henrietta will be visiting a certain puddle. I wish I could stop her, but some children just have to go their own way – that's one thing I've learned about being a mother.